DECEIVED
P9-CCS-753
By

Kidnapped!

Introduction

Volume 4: Death in the Forest

In June 1751, upon his parents' death, 16-year-old **David Balfour** left the small Scotland town of Essendean to travel to "the house of Shaws," the estate of his only living relative, **Ebenezer Balfour**. The uncle proved a greedy old man, living in a huge, decaying old house, who even tried to trick David into falling to his doom from a great height. David had reason to believe that his late father **Alexander** was the older brother and should have inherited the estate.

Ebenezer lured David to the Queensferry docks on the promise he could speak with a lawyer named **Rankeillor**, who knew the Balfour family's history. But Ebenezer had secretly arranged for David to be kidnapped to sea by a **Captain Hoseason** of the Covenant. At sea, the ship struck a small boat, whose only survivor was **Alan Breck Stewart**. Alan was an exiled Scottish Jacobite—one desiring to see the British throne go to James of Scotland, whose supporters had been brutally defeated half a decade earlier. When Captain and crew tried to seize Alan's belt-full of gold, the Scot and David teamed up to seize the ship's main cabin.

Soon afterward, David was thrown overboard amid surging breakers, while the ship was borne away. Reaching civilization, David found messages left by Alan, who with the crew had survived the Covenant's sinking. Following instructions, David proceeded to Alan's homeland. On his way there, he learned that **Colin Campbell**, a nobleman despised by Scots and known as The Red Fox, was about to begin the expulsion of Scottish tenants from their lands. On the road, David abruptly came face to face with four men on horseback—and realized one of them was the infamous "Red Fox"...

Writer: Roy Thomas

Penciler: Mario Gully

Inker: Jason Martin

Colorist: Sotocolor's

A. Crossley

Letterer: David Sharpe

Cover Artist: Gerald Parel

Production: Paul Acerios

Special Thanks –

Sankovitch, Allo, Ginter, Nausedas

Associate Editor: Nathan Cosby

Senior Editor: Ralph Macchio

Editor in Chief: Joe Quesada

Publisher: Dan Buckley

Spotlight

MARVEL®

VISIT US AT
www.abdopublishing.com

Reinforced library bound edition published in 2011 by Spotlight, a division of the ABDO Group, 8000 West 78th Street, Edina, Minnesota 55439. Spotlight produces high-quality reinforced library bound editions for schools and libraries. Published by agreement with Marvel Characters, Inc.

Printed in the United States of America, Melrose Park, Illinois.
042010
092010
This book contains at least 10% recycled material.

Library of Congress Cataloging-in-Publication Data

Thomas, Roy, 1940-
Kidnapped! / adapted from the novel by Robert Louis Stevenson ; adapted by: Roy Thomas ; illustrated by: Mario Gully. -- Reinforced library bound ed.
p. cm.
"Marvel."
Summary: Retells, in comic book format, Robert Louis Stevenson's tale of sixteen-year-old David Balfour who, after being kidnapped by his villainous uncle, escapes and becomes involved in the struggle of the Scottish highlanders against English rule.
ISBN 978-1-59961-781-7 (vol. 1) -- ISBN 978-1-59961-782-4 (vol. 2) -- ISBN 978-1-59961-783-1 (vol. 3) -- ISBN 978-1-59961-784-8 (vol. 4) -- ISBN 978-1-59961-785-5 (vol. 5)
1. Scotland--History--18th century--Juvenile fiction. 2. Graphic novels. [1. Graphic novels. 2. Scotland--History--18th century--Fiction. 3. Adventure and adventurers--Fiction.] I. Gully, Mario. II. Stevenson, Robert Louis, 1850-1894. Kidnapped. III. Title.
PZ7.7.T518Kid 2010
741.5'973--dc22

2009052844

All Spotlight books have reinforced library bindings and are manufactured in the United States of America.

And what seek ye in Aucharn?
The man that lives there.
Ah... James of the Glens.
Is he gathering his people, do ye think, Mungo?
Either way, we'd do better to stay where we are till the soldiers come for us.

If you are concerned for me, I am neither of his people nor yours...
...but an honest subject of King George, owing no man and fearing no man.
Still, what does an honest man so far from his country--
--and seeking the brother of Ardshiel?
I have heard that you were a hard man.
Your tongue is bold, but I am no unfriend to plainness.
If ye had asked me the way to the door of James Stewart on any day but this--

KRAKK
OOHHHH!
T-take care...of your-selves.
I am... dead.
The murderer!
I see him!

I began to scramble up the hill--
--and soon saw a man emerge from a fringe of birches...

Come back here, boy!

Why should I come back?
Come you on!

At that moment, two redcoats joined the party below...
Ten pounds if ye take that lad!
He's an accomplice-- posted here to hold us in talk!

KRAK
KRAK

It was Alan Breck--who stood holding a fishing rod.
Come!
Duck in here among the trees!

Then he set off running...
...and I, like a sheep, followed him.
Quarter of an hour later, he traced back the way we had come, only higher...
You... was a hot burst... David.
Are ye wearied?
I liked you very well, Alan...
But your ways are not mine--and they're not God's--
And the short and the long of it is that we must go our separate ways!
For what reason, Mr. Balfour of Shaws?
You know very well yon Campbell-man lies in his blood upon the road!
If I were going to kill a gentleman, it would not be in my own country, to bring trouble on my clan--
--and I would not go lacking a gun, and with a long fishing rod!
I swear upon the Holy Iron--
--I had neither art, nor part, act, nor thought in it!
Then did you see who shot the Red Fox?
It's a strange thing that I should have been tying my brogues at the time...
...and besides, I've a grand memory for forgetting.

You exposed yourself and me to draw the soldiers.
But if we're caught, I have no fear of the justice of my country.
This is a Campbell that's been killed.
It'll be tried in Inverara, the Campbells' head place...with fifteen Campbells in the jury box...
...and the biggest Campbell of all sitting on the bench.
Justice, David? The same justice as Glenure found at the roadside!
We're in the Highlands, man.
When I tell ye to run, take my word and run.
It's a hard thing to skulk and starve in the heather...but it's harder yet to lie shackled in a redcoat prison.
I'll chance it and go with you, Alan.

You'll lie bare and hard, and brook many an empty belly.
Your bed shall be the moor, and your life shall be like the hunted deer's...
...and ye shall sleep with your hand upon your weapons.
Later, when they stopped to eat and drink...
I left all those messages to bring you to the Appin, after the sea closed over the *Covenant*.
Captain Hoseason was for killing me, but that little man with the red head--
Riach.
He cries to me to run, so I ran, leaving them to quarrel amongst themselves.

Soon, having been supplied with arms and money by Alan's kinsman, James of the Glens, we were on our way again.
Sometimes we walked, sometimes ran...
...and, as it drew on to morning, we walked ever the less and ran the more.
The first peep of dawn found us in a rock-strewn valley where ran a foaming river...
This is no fit place for you and me.
This is a place they're bound to watch.

Look neither to the right nor to the left, David!

Hnnnhh!

Hang or drown, laddie!
HANG OR DROWN!
Unnnhhh...
Never a word he said...

...but set off running again for his life...
...and I must stagger to my feet and run after him...
...till we reached two great rocks that leaned together at the top.
It was only at his third trial that Alan secured a lodgement...
...then pulled me to a place where several men might have lain hidden.
A redcoat camp...half a mile up the river.
We must wait till tomorrow night to try getting by them.
In the afternoon we climbed down into the shade of the rocks...
And, as soon as the shadow of the night had fallen, we started our steep ascent up the mountain.

It was still dark when we reached our destination...
That cleft is the Heugh of Corrynakiegh.
We'll sleep in that shallow cave up there.
Five days we spent there, with Alan teaching me to use my sword...
And I believe he made it more of a pain than need have been.
But you are not to suppose that we neglected our chief business, which was to get away...
I'll leave this "fiery cross," made from last night's embers--with the button I gave you--in the nearby hamlet of Koalisnacoan.
Friends of mine will find it...
...and will know the son of Duncan is in the heather and has need of them.
Alan was troubled when he returned...
The country is alive with redcoats because of the killing of the Red Fox.
My kinsman James has been clapped in prison at Fort William.
It is noised on all sides that I fired the shot...
...and there is a reward of one hundred pounds issued for both ye and me!

Through a friend, my mother besought me not to let myself be captured, or I'm a dead man...
...and she sent what little money she could beg or borrow.
Here's my button back again, and I thank you for parting with it.
More than eleven hours of hard traveling brought us early in the morning to low hills, some red with heather.
Appin's fair death to us, and to the south it's all Campbells... so we'll strike east.
East be it!
But I was thinking, if he would only take one point of the compass, and let me take any other, it would be the best for both of us.
bout noon we lay down o sleep...Alan taking he first watch...
...I, the second.
But I had taste of sleep in my throat...
.and I woke to see that had betrayed my trust.
Alan! Awake!

What...?
Horse soldiers to the southwest...

They're spread out in the shape of a fan...
...and riding their steeds to and fro in the deep parts of the heather...
...looking for us!

We'll have to play at being hares!

They've not spied us...

They're holding straight on!

Come! We must reach yonder mountain.

I... can't go on.

Very well, then.
I'll carry ye.

Lead away!

I'll follow.

We walked all night...
And, came the morning, we were going down a heathery hill...

RUSTLL

YYAAAAAAAAAAAAA

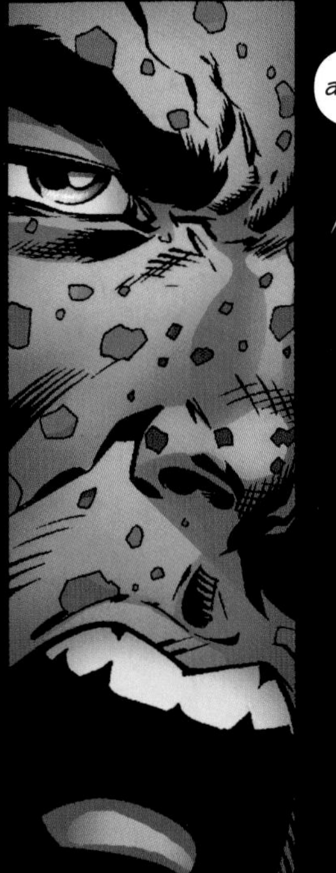

They are Cluny's men!

Cluny Macpherson, chief of the clan Vourich, had been one of the leaders of the rebellion six years before.
We couldn't have fallen better, David.

Cluny will be glad to receive you, Alan Breck Stewart.

uite at the top f the mountain alled Ben Alder, e came to a trange house...
It's known in these parts as Cluny's Cage.
This is but one of his hiding places...while he's rumored to be in France.
But Cluny Macpherson is still in his own country...
...and kept by his own clan.
Well, Mr. Stewart, come away, sir...
...and bring in your friend that as yet I dinna ken the name of.
KOF KOF
And how is yourself, Cluny?
I am proud to see ye...

...and to present to ye my friend the Laird of Shaws, Mr. David Balfour.
I make ye welcome to my house...a queer, rude place for certain... but one where I have entertained a royal personage, Mr. Stewart--
Ye doubtless know the personage I have in my eye.
Here's a toast to ye...
The Restoration!
After we were done eating...
Shall we play a hand or two?
I see little company, and sit and twiddle my thumbs...
I will not judge others... but I fear I eschew card-playing.
What kind of Whiggish talk is this for the house of Cluny Macpherson?
If he has no mind to the cards, it will never hinder you and me.
What with the brandy and the venison, I slept heavily on a corner bed of heather...

luch later, I woke
o see Alan stooping
over me...
David, I'd like a loan of your money.

Wh... what for?
Ye wouldn't grudge me a loan?

I was so weary I slept most of two days...

nd, on the morning
f the third...
My scouts report all clear in the south, boy...

...but have ye the strength to go?
I do not know if I am as well as I should be...
But the little money we have has a long way to carry us.
David...

...I've lost it. There's the naked truth.
My money, too?

You shouldn't have given it to me.
I'm daft when I get to the cards.

Hoot-toot! Hoot-toot! It's all nonsense.
Of course you'll have ***your*** money back, lad!

An evening later, Alan and I were put across Loch Errocht under cloud of night...

...and we went down its eastern shore toward another hiding place near the end of Loch Rannoch.
For long, we said nothing, marching along, each with a set countenance.
I, angry and proud...
...Alan, angry and ashamed.
At last, he could bear it no longer...
David...this is no way for two friends to take a small accident.
I know I was to blame...
Why, of *course*, ye were to blame...
...and you will bear me out that I have never reproached you.
Never! But are we to part?
I'm not very keen to stay where I'm not wanted.
Alan Breck! I never yet failed a friend...
...and it's not likely I'll begin with you.
I will only say this to ye, David...that I have long been owing ye my life...
...and now I owe ye money.
This was a dreadful time, rendered the more so by the gloom of the weather and the country.
I was never warm. my teeth chattered in my head...

And when I slept, with the rain beating above and the mud oozing below me...it was to live over again in fancy the worst part of my adventures...
...to see the tower of Shaws lit by lightning...
...poor Ransome carried below decks...
...Shuan dying on the roundhouse floor...
...or the Red Fox grasping the bosom of his coat.
From such broken slumbers...

...I would be roused in the gloaming...
...to sit up in the same puddle where I had slept.
The third night, as we passed through the country of Balquhidder, a northerly wind blew the clouds away and made the stars bright.
But the change of weather came too late for me, for I was deadly sick and full of pains and shiverings...
Let me get my arm about ye, David.
We'll try that house, though that's no very safe enterpris in such a part of the Highlands.
Chance served us well, for it was a household of Maclarens...
Alan Breck Stewart? Ye are not only welcome for your name's sake...but ye are known by reputation.
My name is Duncan Dhu.
We'll put the lad to bed without delay, and fetch a doctor.

The doctor found me in a sorry plight, yet...
He'll be all right, with a week's bed rest.

All that time, Alan would not leave me, despite the danger to him.
He hid by day in the woods, visiting the house by night...

...while Mrs. Maclaren thought nothing too good for her guests.

And then, early on the evening before the morn when we were to depart...
BAM
BAM
BAM
Who can be so loudly banging upon our door?
'Tis *Robert Oig* himself, of the clan Macgregor!
One of the sons of the notorious Rob Roy!
He had shot James Maclaren at the plough stilts, a quarrel never satisfied...
Yet he walked into the house of his blood enemies as a rider might into a public inn.
I reflected that it was close upon the time of Alan's coming...
...and these two were little likely to agree.
I am given to know, young sir, that your name is Balfour.
David Balfour... at your service.
Ye will scarce have failed to have heard of my father. But what I am come to say is this:
In '45, my brother marched six companies to strike a stroke for the good side.
The surgeon that cured his leg when it was broken at Prestonpans bore the same name as yourself.
If you are his kin, I have come to put myself and my people at your command.
I fear, sir... I know almost nothing of my descent...
Then I shall take my leave.
David...

Yawn!
How are ye feeling tonight, lad?
Alan...we've a visitor...Robert Oig, of the clan Macgregor.
It sticks in mind, Mr. Macgregor, that I am in the country of my friends, the Maclarens.
I think I have heard that you are a man of your sword?
Mr. Stewart, I am thinking!
I did not know ye were in my country, sir.
Unless ye were born deaf, Mr. Macgregor--
--ye will have heard a great deal more than that.
Then you and I will make a match of it!
Next: The End of the Quest